This book is a work of fiction. Any references to historical events, real people, or real places are used fictitiously. Other names, characters, places, and events are products of the author's imagination, and any resemblance to actual events or places or persons, living or dead, is entirely coincidental.

LITTLE SIMON

An imprint of Simon & Schuster Children's Publishing Division • 1230 Avenue of the Americas, New York, New York 10020 • First Little Simon paperback edition January 2015 • Copyright © 2015 by Simon & Schuster, Inc. • All rights reserved, including the right of reproduction in whole or in part in any form. • LITTLE SIMON is a registered trademark of Simon & Schuster, Inc., and associated colophon is a trademark of Simon & Schuster, Inc. • For information about special discounts for bulk purchases, please contact Simon & Schuster Special Sales at 1-866-506-1949 or business@simonandschuster.com. • The Simon & Schuster Speakers Bureau can bring authors to your live event. For more information or to book an event contact the Simon & Schuster Speakers Bureau at 1-866-248-3049 or visit our website at www.simonspeakers.com. • Designed by Laura Roode. • The text of this book was set in Usherwood.

Manufactured in the United States of America 1214 FFG

10 9 8 7 6 5 4 3 2 1

Library of Congress Cataloging-in-Publication Data • Green, Poppy. • The emerald berries / by Poppy Green ; illustrated by Jennifer A. Bell. — First edition. pages cm. — (The adventures of Sophie Mouse ; #2) • Summary: Eight-year-old Sophie learns about some special emerald berries that will make the perfect color for a painting she wants to do, so she asks her friend Hattie to go with her to Weedsnag Way, a part of the forest that is far from home and very frightening. [1. Fear—Fiction. 2. Adventure and adventurers—Fiction. 3. Mice—Fiction. 4. Frogs—Fiction. 5. Squirrels—Fiction. 6. Animals—Fiction.] I. Bell, Jennifer (Jennifer A.), 1977– illustrator. II. Title. PZ7.G82616Eme 2015 [Fic—dc23] 2014013607

ISBN 978-1-4814-2836-1 (hc)

ISBN 978-1-4814-2835-4 (pbk)

ISBN 978-1-4814-2837-8 (eBook)

the adventures of

SOPHIE MOUSE

2

The Emerald Berries

By Poppy Green • Illustrated by Jennifer A. Bell

LITTLE SIMON

New York London Toronto Sydney New Delhi

Contents

chapter 1

Forest Friends

In the heart of Silverlake Forest, a mouse, a frog, and a snake talked and played by a stream. It was just another after-school playdate for Sophie Mouse and her good friends, Hattie Frog and Owen Snake.

Owen was lazily draped over a low-hanging tree branch. He watched as Sophie, sitting on a rock below,

drew in her sketchbook. She was
adding a bee to her garden scene.

"That reminds me of our field trip
to see the honeybee hives!" Owen
said. "It was my favorite part of
school this week."

Mrs. Wise, their teacher at Silverlake Elementary, had taken them to see how honey was made by the worker bees.

"Want to know *my* favorite thing from this week?" called Hattie. She was hopping from lily pad to lily pad.

"It was the visit from Mr. Wallace, the flying frog!"

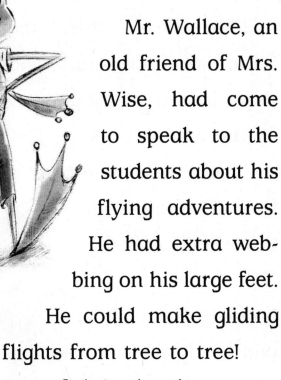

Mr. Wallace, an old friend of Mrs. Wise, had come to speak to the students about his flying adventures. He had extra webbing on his large feet. He could make gliding flights from tree to tree!

Spotting a fish in the clear water, Hattie raced to see if she could beat it to the big rock Sophie was on. "Look at me!" Hattie shouted. "I'm a flying frog!"

Meanwhile, Sophie sketched away, her nose almost touching the paper. She was adding some ants to a log in the foreground. *Maybe one of them should be carrying something,* Sophie thought, *like a seed or a piece of fruit. Ants are so strong!* Sophie

remembered a book she had read once. *It said ants can carry things fifty times heavier than they are. That would be like a mouse carrying a pineapple! I don't think I could carry a pineapple. Plus I don't think I'd want to. The one I saw once in the general store was so prickly looking. . . .*

"Sophie?" Hattie was calling. "Sophie! Hello? Sophie?"

"What?" Sophie replied. She looked up from her drawing. "What did you say?"

Owen and Hattie laughed. "You didn't hear a word we said, did you?" Hattie asked.

Owen added, "I was asking you what *your* favorite part of this week was."

"Oh!" said Sophie. She put her pencil eraser to her chin as she thought it over. "That's easy. Having art class outdoors!"

Mrs. Wise had taught a lesson out-side on Wednesday. It was one part science and one part art. The assign-ment had been to look for different types of mushrooms and draw them.

Sophie loved the outdoors. When she was in school, she liked to sit right next to the schoolhouse window. But Mrs. Wise said it made Sophie too daydreamy. Sophie had to admit: She did love an adventure—even if it was just an imaginary one.

"Haaaar-ri-et!" came a voice from upstream. It was Hattie's mom. She was the only one who called Hattie by her full name. "Anyone over there hungry? I've got a snack for you three!"

Snack? Sophie, Hattie, and Owen looked at one another. Then the race was on to Hattie's house.

— chapter 2 —

A Trip to Town

"Queen me!" Sophie said to her little brother, Winston. They were playing acorn-cap checkers. Sophie already had six queens, while Winston had only two.

It was Saturday morning in the Mouse family's cottage nestled between the roots of an oak tree. Sophie's father, George Mouse, had

lived there all his life. In fact, his grandfather had built the cottage and most of the things inside— including the checkers set Sophie and Winston were using.

Winston's whiskers twitched. He was looking for his next move. He

reached down and double-jumped
two of Sophie's pieces.

Sophie gasped in surprise—then
laughed. "You're getting better,
Winston."

Winston smiled proudly. He was
six. That was two years younger

than Sophie, and he was always trying to catch up.

Just then, they heard their mother,
Lily Mouse, calling from outside. "I
have some errands in town! Anyone
want to come?"

Sophie jumped up. "I do!" she cried.

"But we're not done!" Winston complained.

"We'll finish later," Sophie said, and she dashed to the door. "I promise! Don't let Dad take my place!"

Sophie hardly ever passed up a trip into town. It was only a short walk down the path. But it was a fun change from their sleepy corner of Pine Needle Grove. The library was there, as well as the post office, the

bookstore, and Lily Mouse's bakery, of course.

Today was Lily Mouse's day off, and she had some things to pick up at a few of the other shops.

First, she and Sophie stopped at

Little Leaf Bookstore. Sophie loved the smell of brand-new books.

Mrs. Mouse picked up a pastry cookbook she had ordered. She was famous for coming up with her own unique recipes. But she was always looking for new ideas. "Enjoy!" said friendly Mrs. Follet, the store owner.

Next, they stopped at Handy's Hardware. Mr. Handy, an elderly badger, had put aside some

wooden pegs that Mr. Mouse needed
for a building project.

Then they zipped into the general
store. Mrs. Mouse paid for a tin of
dandelion tea. It went perfectly with

the rolls and cakes at the bakery, so she always liked to have some on hand.

Finally, Sophie and her mom stepped into a tiny shop called In Stiches. The owner, a bluebird named Mrs. Weaver, was the town's

seamstress. Mrs. Mouse had asked Mrs. Weaver to make her a new apron.

"Hello, Lily! Hello, Sophie!" Mrs. Weaver called out as they entered. "Be with you in a moment."

Mrs. Weaver was hemming the skirt of a lovely green silk dress on a hanger.

"Wow!" Sophie cried. "What a color!" The fabric was a deep, shimmery green that had flecks of blue sprinkled throughout. It reminded Sophie of the feathers on a mallard duck.

"Isn't it beautiful?" Mrs. Weaver agreed. She fluttered over to them. "That fabric was dyed with the juice from some very special berries."

Berries? Sophie thought. She had never seen a berry that could make

a color like that. And Sophie knew
her berries. She gathered all kinds
to make different colors of paint for
her paintings.

Sophie needed to get her hands
on some of those berries! *If they*

can make a fabric that color, she thought, *just think what a beautiful paint color they could make!*

"Where do these berries grow?" Sophie asked excitedly.

Mrs. Weaver shook her head. "Oh, nowhere around here, dear," she said.

"Emerald berries grow in *only* one place in the whole wide forest. And it's a place you surely would *not* want to go."

Sophie's brow furrowed. "Why not, Mrs. Weaver?" she asked. She couldn't think of anywhere in the forest she wouldn't go to get berries like that.

Well, except maybe one place. It was a place Sophie had only heard of. It was—

"Weedsnag Way," said Mrs. Weaver.

Sophie gulped.

chapter 3
LIBRARY

Sophie Makes
a Deal

Carrying their packages, Sophie and her mother strolled home. "I think I'll make some dandelion tea and read my new cookbook when we get back," said Mrs. Mouse. "Would you like some tea too, Sophie?"

But Sophie didn't hear her mom. She couldn't stop thinking about the emerald berries. *Oh, why can't*

they grow somewhere other than
Weedsnag Way?

"Sophie?" Lily Mouse said again.

"Hmm?" Sophie said. "Sorry, Mom.
I was just thinking . . . um . . . can
I go over to Hattie's house to play?"

"Oh!" said Mrs. Mouse. "Sure." She
took the wooden pegs
and the apron,

which Sophie had been carrying. "Come home before dinner, okay?"

"Okay!" Sophie called. And she scurried off toward Hattie's house on the stream, while Lily Mouse went on to their cottage.

Sophie *did* want to play with Hattie. She invited Hattie outside to skip stones on the stream. But she also wanted to tell her friend about the emerald berries.

"What?!" Hattie cried when Sophie told her. "Weedsnag Way?" Her eyes went wide with fear.

"*Shhhhhh,*" Sophie said, looking toward Hattie's house. "Keep your voice down. I know, I know. It's supposed to be dark and scary and all that. But I really want to find those berries! We just need—"

"*We?*" interrupted Hattie. "You want *me* to go too? But Sophie, we don't even know how to get there. And it's not just dark and scary. It's supposed to be dangerous and . . ."

As she trailed off, Hattie threw a stone in the stream. She had stopped short of saying one other thing.

Sophie knew what it was. Everyone had heard the story. A squirrel from Pine Needle Grove had ventured to Weedsnag Way once. He'd never come back—and no one had heard from him since.

"But no one *really* knows what it's like," Sophie pointed out. She threw a stone, then turned to face Hattie. "Remember how everyone at school was scared of Owen at first? It was because of all the stories

they'd heard about snakes. Stories that *weren't true*!" Sophie shrugged. "Maybe Weedsnag Way is not really scary and dangerous at all."

Hattie was quiet for a minute. She threw stone after stone into the

stream. Some of them skipped. Some of them just plunked into the water.

Then she spoke. "Are you going to go there no matter what?" Hattie asked.

Sophie smiled. Hattie knew her so well. "If I can find a map," Sophie said.

Hattie sighed. "Then I'll come. But on one condition: If we run into any danger, we turn back. Deal?"

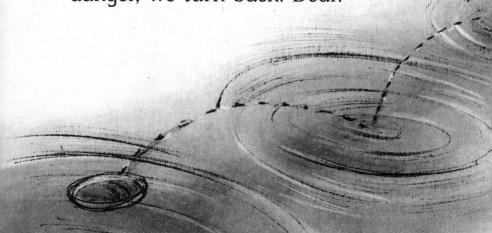

Sophie rolled her eyes, pretending
not to like Hattie's rule. But secretly,
she was relieved. She knew it was a
good idea.

Sophie jumped up. "Deal!"

chapter 4

The Journey Begins

Early the next morning, Sophie added a few more supplies to her sack: a canteen of water, a sweater, a hat, and a scarf. Finally, she tucked in a tin of mint-leaf biscuits. Hattie loved those.

Then, all dressed, with her sack on her back, she paused at the front door of the silent cottage. Everyone else was still asleep. She didn't *want* to tell her parents where she was going. They might say she couldn't go. But it didn't feel right just leaving. So Sophie wrote a note:

Went on a long hike with Hattie. Be back before dark.

Sophie

She left it on the table. *It's not the whole truth,* thought Sophie. *But it's most of it.*

Hattie was waiting outside her front door when Sophie arrived. "Ready?" Sophie asked excitedly.

Hattie nodded, but she looked a little nervous.

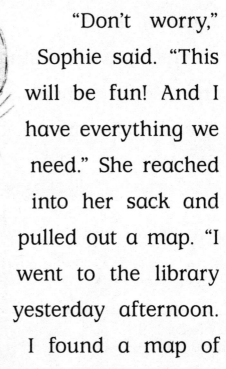

"Don't worry," Sophie said. "This will be fun! And I have everything we need." She reached into her sack and pulled out a map. "I went to the library yesterday afternoon. I found a map of Weedsnag Way and copied it down."

On her hand-drawn map, Sophie had marked the path in red ink.

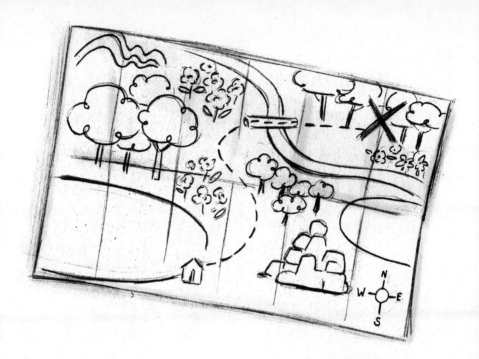

Weedsnag Way had a big red X on it.

Sophie led the way. Hattie followed, slowly at first. But as they walked through familiar woods, Hattie's pace picked up. Soon they were walking side by side, laughing and chatting.

Then they came to the banks of Forget-Me-Not Lake. Hattie stopped. She gazed out at the lily pads on the water. Sophie knew what she was thinking. Hattie wished that *this* was

their destination instead of Weedsnag Way. The friends loved coming to the lake together to hopscotch across the water on the lily pads. But they didn't have time today.

Sophie picked two honeysuckle
flowers from a nearby bush. She
handed one to Hattie. As they walked,
they sucked the sweet nectar from
the inside.

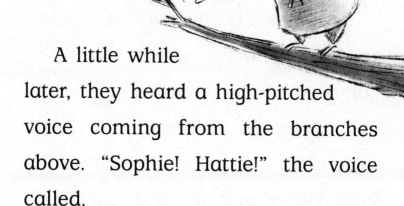

A little while
later, they heard a high-pitched
voice coming from the branches
above. "Sophie! Hattie!" the voice
called.

Sophie looked up. "Zoe!" she cried.
She saw their friend from school flying down to say hello. "I forgot that
your house is over here!"

"Well," said Zoe, "my flightless
friends hardly ever come over to this
side of the lake! I guess it feels too

far from home. But for us birds, it's just a quick flight into town."

Sophie and Hattie laughed. "I guess you're right!" said Sophie. "But we're going *very* far from home today." She explained that she and Hattie were going to try to find Weedsnag Way. "Want to come with us?"

"Oh! Oh, noooo!" said Zoe, flutter-ing nervously. "Weedsnag Way? No, thank you, I do *not* want to come."

And off Zoe flew without another word.

chapter 5

What's That Sound?

"She didn't say she'd ever *been* there," Sophie pointed out.

Hattie didn't reply. The two friends walked on quietly through the woods.

Sophie kept checking the map. "There should be a rocky hillside coming up," Sophie said.

Sure enough, they soon passed a

rise with a rocky face on one side.

"Next we should come to a brook with a big log fallen across it," said Sophie.

There, up ahead, was a babbling brook. The girls used the fallen log as a bridge to cross the water. Their

route took them downstream along the brook. After a while, a large stream joined up with the brook. Now it was more like a river. The water got rougher and faster-moving.

Sophie and Hattie continued on through the woods along the

riverbank. Soon Sophie started to hear a sound. It seemed far off, but it was constant, like a gust of wind blowing on and on.

As they walked, Sophie noticed that the sound was getting louder.

Sophie looked at Hattie. "Do you hear that?" she asked.

Hattie nodded. "What is it?"

Sophie didn't know. But she was curious to find out. She sniffed the air, but all she could smell was the water of the river. She hurried on. The sound got louder . . . and louder . . . and louder. Before long, Hattie had to shout to be heard over the roaring sound.

"SOPHIE!" she cried. "I THINK WE SHOULD GO BACK!"

Hattie had stopped walking. Sophie looked toward the sound, then back at Hattie. She didn't want to go on without Hattie. But she *did* want to know what was making that noise! It felt as if they were so close. The roar almost seemed to shake the ground.

In front of them were some tall

reeds that blocked their view of the way ahead.

Sophie scurried forward a few steps. She parted the reeds and poked her head through.

What she saw took her breath away.

"Hattie! Come look!" she shouted. "You have to see this!"

Hattie hopped over. "Oh my . . ." was all she said.

They were gazing out over a roaring waterfall. The rushing water caught the sunlight and glinted as it fell. Two rainbows made a double arc over the misty pool below.

"I've never seen anything so beautiful!" said Hattie. The fear had

left her face. In its place was a huge
smile.

"Now *this* is an adventure!" said
Sophie.

She pulled out the map to check
their position. She studied it for

several moments. "Huh," she said. "That's funny."

Hattie looked at the map too. "What's funny?" she asked.

Sophie looked up at Hattie. "It's just . . ." she began. "The waterfall. It's nowhere on the map!"

chapter 6

LOST!

Hattie and Sophie backtracked so they could talk without having to shout. Sophie opened her sack. She took out the water and the mint-leaf biscuits. While they nibbled, they looked at the map together.

"You're right," said Hattie at last. "There's no waterfall anywhere on the map." She looked up at Sophie.

"So what do we do now?"

Sophie folded the map. She tucked it back into her sack, along with the water and biscuits. She sniffed the air and looked around. She wasn't really sure which way to go. *But if I tell Hattie that, she'll want to go home,* thought Sophie.

Sophie pointed toward the woods, away from the river. "Let's go this way,"

she said, trying to
sound confident.

Hattie nodded
and followed along.
"Phew!" she said.
"I'm so glad that roar
was coming from a
beautiful waterfall
and not . . . well,
not *something else!*"

They walked and walked, deeper
and deeper into the forest. Sophie
looked up, down, and all around.
She was trying to take everything in.

The trees here are different,

Sophie noticed. She was used to the oak and ash and pine trees in Pine Needle Grove. But these trees were all very tall with smooth, white bark. Hattie seemed to notice too. Now and then, Sophie turned around to find

Hattie studying a tree trunk. The first few times, Sophie didn't think much of it. Then it seemed as if Hattie was stopping more and more. Each time, just as Sophie was about to ask what she was doing, Hattie hurried along to catch up.

"Is it . . . darker here?" Hattie asked after some time had passed. "Or is it just my imagination?"

Sophie looked up. The tall trees and their leaves were blocking out most of the sunshine. "It does seem very . . . *shady*," Sophie said.

They walked on a while longer. A

cold gust of wind blew past. Sophie's teeth started to chatter.

"Is it *colder* here, too?" Hattie asked.

Sophie nodded. "That definitely was a brisk breeze," she said. She pulled her scarf from her sack. She wrapped it around Hattie's neck. "There. Better?"

Nearby, an owl hooted loudly in the trees. Startled, Hattie jumped.

"Sophie, where *are* we?"

Sophie looked down at her map. "I . . . I'm not . . ." Sophie didn't want to say it, but she honestly wasn't sure where they were.

Hattie's look of fear was back, and now Sophie was feeling it too. She checked her sack. They had only a few biscuits left and little bit of water. But worst of all, they were lost! And it was all Sophie's fault! What if they couldn't find their way home?

Sophie couldn't help thinking: Would they end up just like the squirrel in the story?

Just then, there was a rustling in the bushes right beside them. Sophie and Hattie grabbed each other's hands. Too afraid to run, they stood frozen to their spot.

Then they saw it—a bushy gray tail sticking up from behind some leafy branches!

Sophie and Hattie squeezed each other tighter. They kept their eyes glued on the tail as it moved toward them—closer and closer and closer.

~ chapter 7 ~

The Way to Weedsnag Way

With a sudden crack of branches, something with gray fur landed right at Sophie's and Hattie's feet.

"Aaaaaahhh!" they cried. They covered their eyes in fear of the ferocious, monstrous . . .

"Squirrel?" said Sophie, peeking between her hands.

With a flick of his twitchy tail,

the squirrel tilted his head to one side, then smiled a big, friendly smile! "Afternoon! The name's Harry. Harry Higgins. Sorry if I scared you. I couldn't help overhearing. Do you need help finding your way?"

Sophie and Hattie looked at each

other in disbelief—and relief. "Why yes!" Sophie replied. "We could use a little advice."

"Well, well, well," said Harry, "I'm happy to help. I've lost my way before. No fun, no fun. Where are you headed?"

Hattie spoke up. "Have you heard of a place called Weedsnag Way?"

"Where the emerald berries grow?" Sophie added.

Harry Higgins' eyes went wide with surprise. "Emerald berries? Weedsnag Way? *That's* where you're going?"

Sophie got ready for another warning—just like Zoe's.

But she was wrong. Instead, Harry Higgins wiggled his

whiskers and chuckled. "Of course I know how to get there. That's where I live!"

"It *is*?" cried Sophie.

"Are we close?" asked Hattie.

Harry nodded. "Follow me!"

Sophie couldn't believe their luck. She'd been about to give up—to tell Hattie they were lost. But they'd found the perfect guide!

They excitedly followed Harry. He led them down a slope, over a rock pile, through a curtain of weeping willows—and then he stopped.

"Here we are!" he said. "Welcome to Weedsnag Way."

Sophie peeked around him. For the second time that day, she gasped at the sight she saw. Hundreds of emerald-green bushes lined the path on both sides. Long branches arched over the path, making a tunnel. The sparkling berries—dozens on each

bush—made it look like a deep green sky filled with twinkling stars.

Sophie, Hattie, and Harry walked slowly through the arcade. Sophie reached out and picked one of the berries. She squished it between her fingers. The berry juice was a gorgeous shimmering green with blue flecks.

"Perfect!" Sophie cried. "What an amazing paint color this will make!" She explained to Harry how she'd seen a dress dyed with emerald berry juice. "That's why I was so eager to find some."

Harry nodded. "Oh, I understand," he said. "Do you know . . . *I* was drawn here by the emerald berries too. I used to make and sell hats. One day I saw a swan wearing a beautiful hat pin made with emerald berries. I wanted to make one just

like it. So I came out here to find Weedsnag Way."

Harry paused, then added, "Unfortunately, I got a little lost. I found Weedsnag Way. Then I realized I didn't know the way home! Can you believe it?" Harry laughed. "It turned out okay, though. I decided I liked it here very much and wanted to stay." He sighed a small sigh. "But now and then I *do* miss Pine Needle Grove."

Hattie's jaw dropped. Sophie's

eyes went wide. Sophie and Hattie looked at each other.

Harry Higgins was the squirrel from the story—the squirrel who never returned from Weedsnag Way!

— chapter 8 —

Harry Higgins's Home

"Harry!" Sophie exclaimed. "*We're* from Pine Needle Grove too!"

Harry chittered in surprise. "You are?" he cried. "Well, what a day, what a day! Visitors from Pine Needle Grove!" He scurried off down Weedsnag Way. Then he stopped. He turned and waved for Sophie and Hattie to follow. "This calls for tea!

Come, I'll show you my house."

Sophie and Hattie followed Harry halfway down Weedsnag Way. There, a tall tree grew out from the middle of the berry bushes.

Sophie and Hattie watched as Harry scrambled up the tree trunk. When he got up to a large branch, he turned and looked down. "Stand back!" he called.

The girls stepped back as Harry dropped something down. It unrolled

down the length of the
trunk. The end of it came
to rest at the base of the
tree.

"A rope ladder!" Sophie
said in surprise.

"I've been waiting to use
this! Come on up!" Harry
called.

Hattie climbed carefully
up. Sophie followed right
behind her.

"Welcome," said Harry,
standing at the door of his
little squirrel house. It was

built right where the branch and the tree trunk met.

Harry led them inside a comfortable one-room home. Sophie looked around at the tiny wood stove, the handmade table and stools, and the

pine-wood bed with its pine-needle mattress.

"Please, sit!" said Harry. "Make yourself at home while I get the tea going."

But Sophie was too excited to

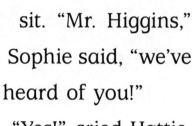

sit. "Mr. Higgins," Sophie said, "we've heard of you!"

"Yes!" cried Hattie. "You're famous in Pine Needle Grove!"

Harry wrinkled his nose. "Famous? Me?" he said. "But . . . what do you mean?"

Together, Sophie and Hattie explained. They told Harry that when he hadn't returned, folks back home decided something very awful had happened to him.

"Everyone thinks Weedsnag Way

is dangerous and scary," said Sophie.

Harry shook his head. "Oh, no, no, no. You two can plainly see. It's not scary at all. It *is* darker, I suppose, because of all the tall trees."

"And colder," Hattie pointed out.

She pulled Sophie's scarf tighter around her neck. "It *is* colder."

Harry nodded. "Perhaps. But I think it's the most beautiful place in the world."

Harry made the tea. Then the three of them sat chatting and laughing.

They imagined what the animals of Pine Needle Grove would say if they could see them at that very moment.

Outside Harry's round window, Hattie noticed the shadows getting longer. "Sophie, I think we'd better start for home."

"You're right," Sophie replied. Then she felt a pang of panic as

something dawned on her.

She didn't know the way home!

Oh, what do I say to Hattie? How can I tell her we're lost—just like Harry?

As if reading her mind, Hattie looked right at Sophie and said, "Don't worry. I know how to get home."

— chapter 9 —

Hattie's Secret

Sophie couldn't believe her ears. "What? You know the way home?"

Hattie nodded confidently.

"But . . . but how?" Sophie asked. Then something occurred to her. "Hattie, did *you* know that *I* didn't know where we were?"

Hattie shrugged. "Not exactly," she said. "But back at the waterfall,

you didn't seem so sure. So just in case, I thought I'd leave a trail." Hattie pulled a handful of long reeds out of her pocket. They were just like the ones at the waterfall. "I tied reeds around some of the thinner tree trunks along the way."

Sophie gasped. So *that's* what Hattie had been doing! She hadn't been studying the trees, after all.

"Hattie, you're a genius!" Sophie

cried. "Now we just need to follow the trail back the way we came."

Hattie nodded. Sophie threw her arms around her and hugged her tight. "Oh, Hattie!" she cried. "Thank you! Thank you for being so careful and practical!"

Hattie's green face blushed pink. "You're welcome," she said with a laugh. Then she turned to Harry. "Mr. Higgins, would you like to come with us? We can take you back to Pine Needle Grove."

Harry thought it over. Then he said, "No, thank you! I don't have any family there. And really, Weedsnag Way is my new home. But you're welcome to come visit me again any time."

Sophie and Hattie smiled. "We will!"

"And when you do," Harry added, "might you bring me something from that wonderful little bakery in town? Perhaps a marigold cupcake with blueberry icing?" Harry rubbed his tummy.

Sophie laughed. "We could do that!" she said. "In fact, I know the owner very well."

chapter 10

The Whole Truth

Passing back through Weedsnag Way, Sophie gathered enough of the emerald berries to fill her pockets *and* Hattie's. Then Harry led them back to the spot where they'd met. The girls said good-bye to their new friend and set off for home.

They had no trouble following Hattie's trail back to the waterfall.

From there, they then followed the river upstream. They crossed the fallen log to the other side. The map showed them the rest of the way home.

Sophie dropped Hattie off at her house. "Do you think anyone will believe what we found in Weedsnag Way?" Sophie asked.

Hattie smiled. "Either way, we know the truth."

Sophie reached her house just

before dark. Inside, she dropped her sack by the front door. Her dad was in the kitchen, cooking dinner—carrot stew by the smell of it. Her mother and brother were on the sofa playing cards. Sophie smiled. She was so happy to be home.

"Well, hello, stranger!" George Mouse called from the kitchen. "That must have been quite a hike. You've been gone all day!"

Sophie hesitated. She knew she had to tell her family about her adventure. Over dinner, she told them the whole story. Her mom and dad listened without saying a word. But Sophie could tell by their

faces, they were not pleased.

"I know," Sophie said. "I should have told you. The map was not right, and we could have gotten lost. I was lucky to have Hattie with me."

Mr. and Mrs. Mouse looked at each other. Sophie got ready for a scolding.

"Please do not ever venture so far off again without telling us," her mother said to her sternly.

"I won't," said Sophie. "I promise."

Mr. Mouse cleared his throat. "And another thing!" he said.

Uh-oh, thought Sophie. *Here it comes.*

But her dad smiled and held out his hand. "Let's have a look at these emerald berries!"

That evening, Sophie tried out her brand-new paint color, emerald berry. She painted a beautiful scene of Weedsnag Way, with a waterfall way off in the distance.

Rising up from the emerald berry bushes was a tree with a rope ladder hanging down the trunk.

And there, at the top of the long
ladder, stood one happy squirrel.

The End

Here's a peek at the next
Adventures of Sophie Mouse book!

Sophie Mouse skipped around the toadstool table. She added a carved-twig spoon to each of the four place settings.

"Napkin on the left, Winston," she told her little brother as they set the table for dinner. "Spoon on the right."

"Oh, right," replied Winston.

"Wait. Which side is left again?"

Sophie tried to be patient as she reminded him. She took a deep breath. Her nose twitched. Her whiskers quivered with glee. Delicious aromas filled the Mouse family's house in the hollow of a big oak tree.

Sophie's father, George Mouse, was at the stove. He was stirring a big pot of radish soup.

Sophie's mother, Lily Mouse, peeked into the oven. She was trying out a new recipe—clover and juniper berry cake.